I0527303

Augustin J. O'Reilly

The Double Triumph

Drama in two acts - Dramatized from the story of Placidus

Augustin J. O'Reilly

The Double Triumph
Drama in two acts - Dramatized from the story of Placidus

ISBN/EAN: 9783337343705

Printed in Europe, USA, Canada, Australia, Japan

Cover: Foto ©Andreas Hilbeck / pixelio.de

More available books at **www.hansebooks.com**

THE

DOUBLE TRIUMPH.

DRAMA IN TWO ACTS.

Dramatized from the story of Placidus, in the "Martyrs of the Coliseum."

BY

A. J. O'REILLY, Mis. Ap.

NEW YORK:

D. & J. SADLIER & CO., 31 BARCLAY ST.

MONTREAL: 275 NOTRE DAME STREET.

1875.

Dramatis Personae.

PLACIDUS, *Roman General.*

IMOGEN,
FARFAX, } *Sons of Placidus.*

RUFUS, *Captain of Banner-Guard. Most faithful friend of Placidus.*

FELIX, *Pope.*

ADRIAS, *Deacon.*

TRAJAN, *Emperor.*

ADRIAN, *Emperor.*

CALPHURNIUS, *High-Priest of the Capitol.*

PROCULUS, *Governor of Gaul.*

EPICURUS, *Manager of Baths.*

SINTULUS, *Military Tribune.*

HIBERNIAN.

STELLA, *Wife of Placidus.*

Soldiers, Lictors, Couriers, Slaves, etc.

THE DOUBLE TRIUMPH.

ACT I.

SCENE 1.—*Rome, second century, time of Trajan. A room in a Roman villa. Matron is sitting at a table working. Two children playing, one about five, the other three years. A slave fanning mistress. After a slight pause a bell is struck outside. Matron calls slave.*

Matron. Sylvia, what hour has struck?

Slave. 'Tis the night-watch, noble mistress.

[*Tramping of soldiers heard outside.*

Matron. What sounds are these? Has Placidus come? Run, Sylvia, and see has the General come.   [*Exit slave.*

Matron [*rising and looking anxiously in the direction whence the sounds came*]. Never has Placidus acted thus. The moon is high in the heavens, and night shrouds the empress city. I see the glare of the vestal fires from the Capitol. [*Looks through lattice.*] Can he be hunting still? This morning at daybreak he left me to greet the rising sun on the Sabines, and chase the swift

3

footed deer.   His hour of return has long passed.
How my heart beats under an anxious pulse!
Ye gods, so propitious to the brave, turn aside
the clouds of evil destiny that might cast a fatal
shadow on the pathway of the Roman! [*Enter*
SYLVIA *hurriedly.*]   Say, Silvia, what tidings?

Slave. Noble mistress, 'tis but the tramp of
the guard changing the night-watch.   But yonder comes Rufus: he surely brings tidings of the
General.

Enter RUFUS. *Soldiers in armor, carrying Roman
banner.*

Matron. Rufus, knowest thou aught of thy
brave commander?   Thou wert ever a true soldier, and kept by his side in the darkest hour.
How came you separated from him?   Speak: I
fear thy silence.   Ye gods, help me! something
has happened.

Rufus. Noble lady, I am loath to fan thy fears
to darker anticipations of evil; but—[*she starts*]
—we fear for the safety of the General.

Matron. I conjure thee, Rufus, to tell me all—
let the worst come, and save me from this rack-
ing suspense.   Have the enemies of the empire
waylaid him?   Has his trusty steed fallen?   Do
ravenous wolves feed on his mangled corpse?

[*She becomes weak, and is led to a chair by
a slave.*

Rufus. Noble lady, none of these calamities has befallen thy lord. Although he separated from us about noon, we believe he has but lost his way in the mountains, and, now that the moon is risen, she will lend her silvery light to guide him to his home.

Matron. But how came you to lose him, Rufus? What happened?

Rufus. Early this morning I was by his side, when a noble stag started from the copse at our feet; the dogs gave chase, and our neighing steeds flew over the mountain-side. The stag was the largest ever seen in those hills, and the chase the fleetest ever run; our jaded horses soon lagged behind, but the General followed on in all the ardor of the chase; we saw his burnished helmet rolling like a globe of fire through the olive-groves, and then appearing at intervals like gleams of moonlight through the ravines of Marino; finally we lost sight of him. We halted in the shade of a fig-tree, and hoped each moment to see our gallant commander return with the spoils of his brilliant chase. Four weary hours passed, and not even a dog returned to tell by his blood-stained mouth of the death of the stag. We then searched the mountain-side, and called aloud again and again for our General; but the echo of our hoarse voices broke the stillness of the mountain-side, mingling with the moan of the startled owls. The setting sun, falling in clouds of golden splendor over the towers of Ostia, made us tremble for his safety. We hurried to head-quarters to seek a detachment of horse to scour the mountain-side. Behold, noble lady, how I am separated from the General! The life-stream of my heart is not dearer than thy lord. Rufus will not wield his battle-axe under any other commander. Placidus must be found!

Matron. Noble Rufus, haste to the Sabines once more, bring back my Placidus, and my gratitude shall dictate thy reward.

[*Noise is heard outside. Soldiers cheer.* SYL-VIA *runs out. All look in the direction.*

Matron. What has happened?

[SYLVIA, *running in, cries out in loud voice.*
Slave. 'Tis Placidus! 'Tis Placidus!

Enter PLACIDUS, *a Roman general, gorgeously dressed, armor, plumes, etc. Embraces his wife. A pause.*

Matron [*emphatically*]. I breathe again. My troubled heart has leaped from despair to joy. Placidus, art thou ill? . . . What has caused this delay, and to thy Stella such long hours of anxious suspense?

[PLACIDUS, *relieving himself from her embrace, slowly passes to a seat; places his head in his hands; seems in trouble. All gather round. After a short pause he rises slowly, waves his hand majestically, making sign for all to depart except matron.* RUFUS, SYLVIA, *soldiers, etc., retire* R. C., *looking anxiously towards him. Again* PLACIDUS *becomes absorbed in thought. At length matron draws near, and, kneeling at his feet, speaks anxiously.*

Matron. Placidus, speak to thy Stella. What cloud hangs on thy cheerful spirit? Never before hast thou come home in this mood; we for hours have watched and turned the hour-glass, listening for thy well-known footsteps on the threshold; but Rufus told us how thou hadst lost thy way in the mountain, and truly prophesied the waning moon would bring thee home. Speak, and let an anxious spouse share thy trouble.

[PLACIDUS, *raising his head and taking his wife's hand, speaks slowly and majestically.*

Placidus. Stella, I have a strange tale to tell thee. Thou knowest the terrors of war and the crash of empires have ever been my delight. I feared no enemy, and knew no god but my sword. Since last I sat beneath these ancestral towers a change has come over the spirit of my dream. Like sunshine bursting from clouds, a vision from the realms beyond the grave has passed before these eyes. A deity greater than the gods of the empire has manifested himself to me. Stella, I am this day a Christian !

Matron. Placidus! art mad ?—that hated sect —persecuted by the emperors—the enemies of the gods ! Think of thy wealth—thy fame—thy children—

Placidus. Hold, Stella! thou must hear me then thou too wilt be Christian. This morning I went as usual to the chase. Never did a more beautiful sun rise over the Campagna—never did fresher breezes blow over the Sabine slopes. I felt all the vigor of youth, and, whilst my steed neighed with impatience, I cursed the gods we could not find the game. Towards the eleventh hour we heard a rustling in the brushwood ; out sprang a magnificent stag ; we gave chase ; we flew over the mountain-side with a speed that would mock the eagle's flight ; torrents rolled under the hoofs of the horses, and fearlessly we rode along the edge of startling precipices ; soon my gallant steed outstripped my companions in the chase. On we went, over hill and dale, and penetrated far into the rocky Apennines. I lost control of my foaming steed, but feared not, for some destiny seemed to urge us on. Suddenly the stag came to bay, made an immense bound, and reached a ledge of rocks that hung over us :

it turned towards me, and, behold, I saw a strange
sight! In its branching horns there was a light
brighter than the sun; my dazzled eyes could
discern in this light the figure of a man nailed to
a cross, who spoke to me words of strange mystery. At the same time a light shot through
my soul—I understood the mercy of the mighty
Being who is alone the true God! [*Pauses, and
fixes his eyes in serious thought on heaven. Then,
starting, suddenly continues.*] Stella, this night
we go to the Catacombs; the pastor Felix, the
chief of the Christian sect, awaits us; he will
explain all. Awaken thy infants, take them with
thee, for a messenger awaits outside to guide us;
ere the dawn of the morrow's sun, we shall be
Christians.

Matron [*excitedly*]. But, Placidus!

Placidus. Hush!

" Procastination is the thief of time,
    Year after year it steals until all is fled,
    And to the mercies of a moment leaves
    The vast concerns of an eternal scene."

[*Matron leaves* L. C. PLACIDUS, *moving slowly after, is called by* SINTULUS, *a military
tribune, who has entered by* R. C.

Sintulus. Placidus, the Emperor expects you
this evening at the Baths of Titus, to meet the

Prefect of the Gaulish Provinces, who has arrived in the city to-day.

Placidus. Sintulus, Placidus is called by a higher power, and will return anon.

[*Exit* L. C.

Sintulus [*looking after him in wonder*]. What mean these words? Called by a higher power than the Emperor! He is plotting a conspiracy. [RUFUS *steals in from behind, unseen by* SINTU-LUS, *and listens.*] What a splendid chance for me to seek promotion by revealing the plot to the Emperor. I shall meet Trajan at the baths, and rise to eminence on the blighted fame of Rome's greatest man. [*Exit excitedly.*

Rufus [*with hand in sword*]. Caitiff! thy first word against Placidus shall be thy last!

[*Remains in attitude of attack. Curtain falls.*

SCENE 2.—*Crypt in Catacombs. Table, large cross, rude and black; on the table, book, hour-glass, etc. Sitting near the table, the* POPE FELIX, *a venerable old man, long white beard, etc.*

Felix. How wonderful are the ways of God! Too mysterious for the grasp of human reason. All is now darkness and gloom, yet triumph is certain. Wrapt in the womb of futurity, truth will emerge like sunrise over the ancient hills on the darkened plains. That Spirit which brooded over the chaotic darkness and illumined creation with the flood of daylight shall utter another fiat over the moral night of paganism, and give Christianity a cloudless sky for the salvation of man. Seventy years have rolled their trying and bloody vicissitudes over thy infant Church since she first sought the shelter of these crypts ; the martyred heroes who sleep in those crimsoned tombs cry to thee for that mercy which is the revenge of a God. Steadily thy holy cause is progressing against the tide of human passions ; each drop of blood that purples Roman soil is the fruitful germ of souls that spring to life under the sword that gives death. Still thy servants bleed in the amphitheatre ; their mira cles dazzle thousands without bringing conviction. The irrational brute sees thy image in the Christian victim ; but man, thy loved creature, is shrouded in voluntary darkness. [*He kneels.*] " How long, O Lord, wilt thou not have mercy on Jerusalem ! " Give one propitious glance on this impious city, and let the voice of thy praise ring through its habitations.

[*After a slight pause he stretches his arms in surprise, and gazes on a vision made to appear on the stage thus : In the centre of the scene there is a second smaller one, which is made to rise slowly. Within is a scene in the Apennines, mountains made with cork. On a rock a stag's head, in its branching horns a crucifix, on which a strong light is reflected from above by a mirror. Under the rock* PLACIDUS, *dressed as in* 1st *scene. A shower of golden snow, made by small slips of gold-paper. Soft music all the time. Curtain falls slowly again. Then a plaintive air is sung without words by a female voice from within, pianissimo.* FELIX, *with hands folded in prayer, the moment the air is sung, springs excitedly to his feet.*

Felix. Have idle fancies been mocking my eyes? What can mean this strange vision? Is it a wile of Satan to distract my thoughts? Ah! thanks to the Eternal Giver of all good gifts, the martyrs bleed not in vain! Behold, an apostle is called, whose conversion shall bring a harvest of souls as numerous as the flakes of golden snow seen in my dream!

Enter ADRIAS, *a young deacon, bearing dalmatic, as was the custom in those times. (N. B. The dalmatic was originally a pagan costume.) Kisses* POPE'S *hand, kneels.*

Felix. My child, what news from the outer world?

Adrias. Holy Father, I have just been to the city, and administered the holy mysteries to the poor family near the Arch of Dollabella ; but I should have been here much sooner were it not that I waited to witness a scene the most glorious in these days of triumph for the Church of God.

Felix. Say, Adrias, what has been thy happy lot ? Has the storm of persecution ceased to toss the bark of truth on the pagan world ? Has man wearied to war with the Great Eternal, and proclaimed the freedom of the unoffending Christian ?

Adrias. Alas ! Holy Father, darker than ever are the clouds that lower on our horizon ; the persecution has freshened to a gale ; the city rings with blasphemy against the crucified God of the Christians. When I crossed the Capitol and descended the Way of Triumph into the Forum, I saw crowds of people engaged in excited conversation. I listened, and learned the edicts against the Christians were to be pushed forward with greater vehemence than ever, and on the portals of the Temple of Fortune I saw and read the bronze plates that announced the crown for so many soldiers of Christ. Suddenly turning towards the Tullian keep, I saw a crowd of brutal men leading in bonds my little friend Marinus. [*Sheds tears.*] Groans, hisses, and shouts burst from the crowd as they led him towards the Coliseum; but the brave child looked tranquil and happy. ' At first impulse I was about to rush to his side and claim companionship in his happy lot. I knew he was going to his crown, and, working my way through the crowd, I whispered encouragement into his ears. He smiled in joy, and bade me bring his last farewell to you. Arrived at the Coliseum, I found its mighty womb already filled with the heartless mob who gloat over the bloody games of the circus; but, wishing to see the end of the noble boy, I wrapped my cloak around me, and took my place in the second tier. A murmur rose through the assembled multitude that a noble Christian youth was to be exposed to the lions. After a moment's pause Marinus was led into the arena; he still bore his senatorial laticlave, and seemed a little seraph in human form. There burst from the people a shout that rolled like thunder through the vomitories of the mighty amphitheatre, and shook the heavens with unutterable blasphemies against God. The trumpets were sounded, and an enormous lion bounded into the arena; he crouched, prepared to spring on the defenceless youth: the silence of death hung over the crowd, when—all praise be to our good Lord!—the animal suddenly drew up, as if some invisible being stayed his ravenous nature; coming gently towards Marinus, the lion commenced to lick the hands and feet of the martyr boy. Cries of witchcraft, of death, and of surprise again moved the crowd. Some called for more animals, others for his liberty, and from not a few I heard the pleasing cry of " Great is the God of the Christians ! "

Felix. What did they then ? Say on, Adrias : was Marinus crowned ?

Adrias. Yes, Holy Father, the prefect was fired with rage, and, fearing a tumult amongst the people, ordered the noble youth to be beheaded. I saw the axe fall. Marinus slept where Ignatius fell, smiling on his murderers with angelic forgiveness ; his body was cast into the spoliarium. I bribed the keepers to give it to me, and I have just committed the sacred relics to the Fossores.

Felix. Poor Marinus ! lovely, angelic boy ; but yesterday you told me how you longed for your crown. Peerless lily of Eden ! transplanted from the gardens of earth to bloom in everlasting fragrance in the blossoms of thy unfading merit. I see thee hailed by millions of kindred spirits, whose smiles of congratulation lendeth lustre to thy well-earned crown. See, Adrias, to the Acts of the noble youth ; let future generations know the material on which the Church of God is built.

Adrias. I have yet another strange circumstance to tell your Holiness, if I may speak.

Felix. Go on, Adrias; everything concerning my persecuted flock must needs interest me. "Who is scandalized and I not burn?"

Adrias. When I was coming along the Salarian Way, bringing with me the relics of Marinus, there suddenly came up a party consisting of two men, a woman, and two children; they seemed beautifully dressed, and one of the men was girded with armor and sword, and seemed to be a military man of high rank. A youth of heavenly appearance, who seemed to guide the party, came towards me, and, saluting the remains of Marinus, called me by my name, and bade me guide the family to you, and instantly disappeared.

Felix. How strange! What did you with the family, Adrias? Where are they now?

Adrias. May it please your Holiness, when I arrived at these Catacombs, not wishing to abandon the body of Marinus till in the safe-keeping of the Fossores, I prayed the priest Cyprian to speak to them until I could acquaint you of the circumstances.

Felix. Haste, Adrias, and bring them to this crypt. [*Exit* ADRIAS.] 'Tis the harvest of blood: the sunshine of eternal truth, struggling through clouds of human darkness, has fallen on a few chosen souls.

Enter PLACIDUS *and family. All kneel. The* POPE *stretches his hands over them in silence for a moment, then, advancing towards them, says :*

Felix. Rise, Placidus! thy name is written in the Book of Life.

Placidus [*slowly and majestically*]. He who rules the destinies of man has deigned to illumine my darkened senses. By divine command I stand before thee, venerable Pastor of the Christian Church, to receive the Sacrament of regeneration.

Felix. My son, dost thou believe?

Placidus. I believe.

Felix. Then hearken to the word that has been spoken in vision to me, the unworthy servant of the servants of God. Great things are destined for thee, Placidus, but thou must first be humbled and proved in the crucible of trial and purified, as dross is taken from the alloy. Go again with the morrow's sun to the spot in the Apennines where the Divine Spirit has manifested itself to thee, and thou wilt hear again the will of him to whom thou pledgest fealty. Nerve thy spirit for greater battles than those that have girded thy name with terror to the enemies of the Empire; thou must fight with enemies invisible, imperishable, and implacable; but all battles are triumphs under the banners of the Son of God. [*Thé chanting of psalms is heard in the distance.*] But hither come our flock for morning prayer; let us repair to the chapel for instruction and baptism.

> [*A procession is then made to pass. Christians in ancient costume, carrying lighted tapers, singing some plaintive chant. A splendid opportunity for a beautiful chorus, such as from the cloister-scene of "I Puritani." After procession,* STELLA, *children,* POPE, *and* PLACIDUS *join and exeunt. Curtain falls.*]

———

SCENE 3.—*Room, as in first scene.* PLACIDUS *sitting at table. Parchment, style, etc.* CALPHURNIUS, *the high-priest of the Capitol, stands before him.*

Placidus [*scornfully*]. What brings you here to-day, Calphurnius?

Calphurnius. A matter of the deepest importance; but first I must tell of my pride in the friendship of Rome's greatest General—the most devout to the gods—

Placidus. There is some villanous scheme lurking under thy lying tongue, but I will hear thee, priest. Thou choosest to be friends with the great. Were I poor and nameless as a slave, would this honor be conferred on me?

Calphurnius. Noble General! the high-priest of the Capitol would not demean his dignity by noticing slaves and serfs, except to trample them under his heel as he would the worm on his path!

Placidus. Enough, proud hypocrite, of thy time-wasting self-stilting! I would hear thy business!

Calphurnius. You are aware, General, the whole empire is groaning under the weight of an increasing misfortune—worse than the failure of the harvest—worse than epidemic or decimating plague—worse than defeat in battle and the subjugation of the empire to a barbarous power—'tis the spread of the Christian sect! [PLACIDUS, *rising, scowls, and places his hand on sword.*] The remedy to this evil, General, is in your hands. Yesterday, when passing through the camp, we heard your name on every soldier's lips, and my colleagues and myself, who are the next power to the army, have agreed in council to get rid of the imbecile emperor who tolerates this impious sect, and place on his throne the chosen of the army, the beloved of the gods—you, Placidus, who will persecute to the death the worshippers of the Jewish Prophet.

Placidus [*slowy and majestically*]. " And leading him up a hill, showed him all the kingdoms of the earth; and said, All these will I give thee, if, falling down, thou wilt adore me." Calphurnius! I would not shed one drop of innocent blood for fifty empires. Would piety towards the gods make me deluge Rome with its noblest blood, and make Roman homes resound with the cry of the widow and the orphan? The Christians are an innocent people; they have the right of citizenship as well as you or your motley crew of pampered hypocrites; but, proud priest, thou art a spider strangled in thy own web; thou hast quaffed the cup thou hast poisoned for an innocent victim; you stand before me a convicted criminal; thou hast conspired against the life and throne of the Emperor, and before sunset thy guilty head shall roll from the public scaffold. Ho! there, guards! [*Enter soldiers, who seize him.*] Calphurnius, I am a Christian!

Calphurnius [*falling on his knees, crying piteously for mercy*]. Mercy! mercy! great General! I only meant—

Placidus. Silence, hypocrite! Calphurnius, thy life is now in my hand; but, as we Christians do not trample on the worm in our path, I will let thee live if thou wilt swear, and sign with thy blood, a compact that thou wilt never again speak against the Christians.

Calphurnius. I swear! I swear!

Placidus. Thou wilt sign, caitiff, thy own death-warrant. [PLACIDUS *goes to table and writes. After writing a moment, during which high-priest is wringing his hands—*] Soldier, tie his finger, and pierce it with this style. Let him sign in blood an oath we will make him keep. [*Soldier ties, etc. High-priest led to table. Refuses.* PLACIDUS *draws sword, and aloud.*] Priest, sign! [*Priest signs.*] Lead the caitiff to the street, and set him free again on the world he contaminates.

Enter RUFUS.

Placidus. Ho, Rufus! we have had a merry time of it just now. You know Calphurnius, the many-colored hypocrite that pretends to wield the thunders of Jupiter—he wanted to make me emperor; the army would proclaim me, and he would secure the consent of the Senate and people if I would promise to persecute the Christians! but I made him swear and sign with his blood a promise never to speak again against the Christians—

Rufus. Better you should have roasted him at his own fires; Calphurnius's oath, even signed with blood, will break like a rotten reed at the first pressure. Thou hast set free, General, a wretch who will move heaven and earth to ruin thee.

Placidus. The conscious heart that fears not the light of day shall little brook the treachery of a miscreant like Calphurnius!

Rufus. Thou hast other enemies, General, more powerful than Calphurnius. Was Sintulus here this morning?

Placidus. Yes, but I dismissed him summarily, as urgent domestic affairs called me.

Rufus. And I overheard him prepare a charge of conspiracy against thee.

Placidus. What! dishonor! Is he in league with the vile Calphurnius—would Trajan believe?

Enter messenger excitedly.

Messenger. General, your villa on the Nomentan Way has been burnt; horses, cattle, and some of the slaves lost!

Placidus [*majestically*]. When the tide of destiny has returned to its rocky boundary, the billows of misfortune flow in steadily, one by one, bearing on their snowy crest the fragments of the storm's wreck! Rufus, my night of long, bitter woe is gathering its sable darkness around me. With shattered fortunes and blighted honor I shall not wait to meet a traitor's doom. [*Enter* ADRIAS, *the deacon, presenting letter to* PLACIDUS. PLACIDUS *opens and reads.*]

" We caution thee, our beloved son Placidus,. of the pagan priest Calphurnius. He has laid a plot to get you to acknowledge yourself a Christian, and then betray you to the Emperor. The rumors of your conversion are passing through Rome. We recommend you to secrete yourself till the storm blow over.   FELIX."

[*A trumpet is heard outside. A courier from the royal household enters.*

Courier. The Emperor would have the General Placidus to meet him at the Temple of Apollo,. on the Palatine, before sunset.   [*Exit.*

Placidus. The hour is not yet come in which I must proclaim my faith to all the Roman people, but the fire around the crucible into which my sinful nature is to be cast is reaching a blaze. Rufus, take this scroll, and, if avenging Heaven place it in thy power to vindicate the sanctity of an oath, let retributive justice mete that caitiff's doom. Be heir of my horse and my faithful dog—they may no more accompany their master to the chase ; take my sword [*unbuckles belt*] ; other weapons must be wielded against enemies that are invisible, indestructible, and implacable. [*moves towards lattice.*] Farewell, thou mighty city, whose monuments of a thousand victories are the soldier's pride! whose legions are the terror of every nation ! whose dark idolatry is the regret of every Christian! Farewell, thou marble walls of my ancestral home—thy softening memories shall haunt my exile and embitter the hardships of my servitude. And to the veteran companions of our arms, thou, Rufus, must tell them their General [*weeps*]—struggles to say—farewell!

[SCENE.—*Agonies of farewell by* PLACIDUS, *gradually receding. Sudden exit. Rufus in grief. Curtain falls. Music plaintive and pianissimo during the silent farewell of* PLACIDUS.

SCENE 4.—*A hall in the Baths of Titus.* EMPEROR *on throne. Around, courtiers, gold cups in their hands, all gorgeously dressed.* (*The dress of* TRAJAN, *as taken from his statue in Rome, given in Goldsmith's "History of Rome."*) *Enter* EPICURUS, *a red-faced noble, who glories in the title of Bagnanius, or Manager of the Baths.* EMPEROR *seeing him approach.*

Trajan. Ha, Epi! you have been lifting your Falernian cups rather freely this afternoon. I could hear your merry laugh the loudest in the triclinium whilst we were swimming.

Epicurus. Most divine Emperor! I—I am the happiest man in this mighty realm!

Trajan. What has happened, then, to make you more so than usual?

Epicurus. Plenty, by Jupiter! Yesterday one of my saw-mill wives had her threads cut and slipped down to the infernal home of Pluto; to-day I had a meeting of creditors who agreed to let me go free from what they knew they never would get; and I have here [*seizing a silver jug placed on a table in the centre*] the finest ten-year-old vintage, the taste of which would make old Bacchus thirsty every time he would pass a tavern. [*All drink.*

All. Remarkably good; very fine wine indeed!

Epicurus [*aside*]. Mighty fine judges indeed!

[*Makes gestures to show the pump had something to do with it. Whilst they are drinking a trumpet is heard outside.*

Epicurus. Here comes Proculus, the prefect of the Gaulish Provinces! [*Enter, rapidly,* PROCULUS, *a military commander. Sword, plumes, cloak, etc. Kneels at Emperor's throne.*]

All. Hail to the conqueror of the Britons!

Proculus. Most Supreme Emperor, pardon my late appearance at the imperial audience.

Trajan. Rise, Proculus, and relate at ease the history of thy travels, thy battles, and thy conquests. Fill thy glass, Proculus, and drink some of Epi's ten-year-old.

Epicurus [*aside*]. 'Tis not mine now ; I'll never
see it again !

> [*They drink.   A verse of some popular song
>   may be here introduced ; we would suggest
>   one of Prout's adaptations in Latin to the
>   airs of " Moore's Melodies."*

Trajan. And now, Proculus, what think you
of the Bretons?

Proculus. Most divine Emperor, I swear by my
sword a braver or nobler people never yet passed
under the Roman yoke.* We are victorious, but
our victory has cost us the flower of our legions.
For several months we carried on an unequal war-
fare. The hardy race made impregnable fortresses
of their mountains, and forced us to loiter and
starve in uncultivated plains.   At length we
called to our aid the stratagem that defeated the
invincible Troy of old. We feigned a retreat. The
hardy warriors rushed from the mountains, yelling
a victorious war-whoop, and followed us with fatal
indiscretion to the plains. We suddenly turned
our front and gave them battle, but the veterans
of thy armies were matches. For three long days
a bloody battle raged, and I feared at one time
the combat would end with nothing short of the

---

* The yoke was a species of wooden arch (sometimes square),
under which a conquered army was made to pass in token of
their defeat and degradation.

annihilation of both armies. At length I deter-
mined by a desperate blow to close the engagement. Seeing their brave chieftain on a white
charger, leading on his comrades in the thick of
the fight, with all the ardor of my youthful days
I rushed for him, and engaged him at once in a
desperate struggle. The two armies by mutual
accord remained with uplifted swords to watch
the issue of our deadly combat. We fought and
struck and parried for an hour. Both our horses
were slain at the same moment, we grappled each
other, and fell in a pool of blood. I heard a faint
cry from my veterans, and with one desperate
effort I plunged this poniard into his heart!
[*Shows poniard still stained with British chieftain's blood. All present cheer.* PROCULUS *continues.*] The battle was now over, and whilst I
was carried to my tent, bleeding and faint, I
heard from the rejoicing veterans of my army the
well-known cry of their victory. Peace could be
had from this brave people only under one condition—that their sons and daughters should not
be seized as the slaves of the Roman people.
Fearing the issue of a second engagement with a
maddened and despairing nation, and admiring
the nobility of character that placed our new al-
lies in a standard of honor equal only to Rome
itself, I signed, with a trembling hand, a treaty
the most glorious in the archives of war. Most

noble Emperor! it ill becomes me to laud the importance of the conquest benign Fortune has given for my boast; but conviction bears me over the gulf of centuries to behold in the march of nations the future glory of Britannia. The tutelary duties of our wealth, our civilization, and our power will meet the sweep of Boreas in their progress to the North, and build up their celestial thrones in that part of the firmament whence they can smile on the land of the Briton. A people so brave, so industrious, so noble, have a power more lasting than an impregnable fortress, or an empire that can guard her frontier with a girdle of steel. When our superb city, now the mistress queen of the world, shall have grown old and feeble; when the golden grains of her brilliant career shall have ceased to run in the glass of time, she will pass to ruin like Troy, like Carthage and Athens; but the manes of her fallen magnificence shall flee to the land whose natural wealth and moral worth shall give her a new empire to rule. And now, emperor, I ask but one favor: Weakened with wounds and bowed with age, may this laurel wreath which my triumph has placed on an unworthy brow, be never again ruffled by the storms of war; may its withered leaves be never replaced by fresh tokens of the bloodshed and slavery of a free people!

[Approaches and lays his sword at the foot of Emperor's throne. Kneels in silence, etc.

Trajan. Proculus, I know not which to admire most—the bravery that has won for the empire such valuable conquest, or the magnanimity that makes thee place thy sword at our feet. Although great the loss of your guiding spirit to our invincible legions, it would be cruel and unjust to refuse the retirement you so justly deserve. Share, then, for the rest of thy days the splendors of our golden house, and leave the art and cruelty of war to the young and ambitious, whose love of glory is stronger than their sympathy. Rise, General, and be seated near us to assist in the administration of justice. *[Rises and takes place prepared near Emperor.]* And now, Epi, who is the next on your list seeking the honor of an interview?

Epicurus. Calphurnius, may it please your divinity! the well-beloved of the gods—the priest of Jupiter, high-priest of the Capitol, and *[aside]* a whining old hypocrite!

[Whilst last line is being said two boys appear at R. C., entering backwards—dressed as acolytes, bearing pans of burning incense, and salaaming with right hand. Then CALPHURNIUS—dressed in red, yellow, and blue

—fantastically carries small idol of Jupiter in hands. Kneels before EMPEROR.

Trajan. Well, Calphurnius, what's troubling you now more than piety?

Calphurnius. Divine Emperor! worse than a thousand deaths, the piety towards the gods is waning; the detestable Christian sect is increasing, and their wily old chief is sapping the foundations of thy imperial throne! [*There would be a fine opening here to introduce an extract from some ranting declaimer against papal aggression.*] Down in the crypts of the Vatican this rival monarch holds his meetings. Some of the noblest families of the city go there to worship a calf's head and drink the blood of a murdered child. In the name of the immortal gods whose temples are abandoned, in the name of the priests whose feasts and fees are becoming reduced, we wish to have renewed the salutary laws of our beloved and divine Nero. Add to thy many deeds of valor and glory, a name which shall be handed to posterity for piety towards the gods, in the annihilation of the Christian sect!

Trajan. Calphurnius, besides the fact of lessening your fees, can you say wherefore those Christians may not be permitted to live?

Calphurnius. Permit them to live, Emperor, and you shall be the first victim of their dark conspiracies. Already your throne is shaken ; from the provinces there comes a cry of indignation at your ill-starred leniency towards those enemies of mankind ; by your toleration they have increased like vermin in an unswept chamber ; the army is contaminated, and the plebs are fascinated with the unheard-of charity they practise towards one another. Fearing their increasing power and numbers, we announce to thee, Emperor, unless thou persecutest to the death those hated Christians, the robes shall be torn from the priests of the immortal gods, and the time-honored constitutions of this mighty empire shall be forever destroyed. Thy throne shall pass to another, and thyself made the footstool of a Christian.

Trajan. Insolent priest ! the lictors' rods shall teach thee to respect our piety towards the gods. Lictors, see that Calphurnius remains, and when we have ceased our audience we shall interview this noisy priest.

Calphurnius. Mercy, great, immortal Emperor ! There breathes not a more loyal subject to thy majesty than the *pious* Calphurnius !

Enter COURIER.

Courier. Emperor ! Sintulus, the Tribune of the Pretorian Guard, seeks an audience. He has most important news to communicate.

Trajan [*crossly*]. Let him come forward, then, without delay.

[*Enter* SINTULUS. *Kisses ground before throne.*

Trajan. Say, Sintulus, what important business brings thee here to-day?

Sintulus. Emperor, as I live, the gods have made me the happy instrument to save thy life.

Trajan. How, Sintulus?

Sintulus. I have discovered a most dangerous conspiracy against thy throne—

Trajan. Go on, miscreant, or by the gods we will wring from thee thy unpleasant news!

Sintulus. This very evening thy blood would be shed at the vestibule of the golden house, if I were not the most faithful of thy subjects to hasten with warning of the threatened danger. Not many hours ago I overheard the plot : another emperor is already named, and one of thy generals has proclaimed allegiance to the revolution.

Trajan. Who is it that would thus tamper with our royal power? Name him, Sintulus, that the dogs may feed on his carcass by moonlight!

Sintulus. 'Tis no other than the great General Placidus!

Trajan. Placidus!

All. Placidus! Placidus

[*A murmur passes for a moment.* TRAJAN *rises, advancing excitedly :*

Trajan. Ye gods! Placidus plotting my life! Placidus a conspirator! 'Tis false! Miscreant, thou liest like a slave! There's no more honorable blood in the empire than flows in the veins of the brave General!

Sintulus. I swear by the stars shining in the blue vault of heaven, I heard the General say he had now to give his allegiance to a higher power!

Calphurnius. 'Tis true, Emperor; and more, I can testify he is a Christian.

Trajan. Summon the Pretorian guard instantly. Sound the call to arms, and let me meet in battle the wretch that would strike in the dark!

[*Short blast on trumpet. A bustle at* L. C. *Enter* RUFUS *quickly, wrapped in cloak and in disguise. In coarse, rough voice :*

Rufus. Stand aside, Sintulus! I'll deal with thee just now. [*Turning to the Emperor.*] Noble Emperor! there is a foul plot afloat to blast the fame of Rome's greatest man. These statements are false! Would you give credence to the word of a wretch, who would break a sworn oath sealed by his own blood?

Trajan. What mean you, stranger? This is no time for useless queries.

Rufus. One of these witnesses, that has accused Placidus of treason, has himself plotted against thy throne, and offered to make the General emperor. Placidus scorned the power that would be given by dishonorable means; but under his sword made the wretch sign an acknowledgment of his guilt in his own blood!

Calphurnius [*greatly excited whilst Rufus is speaking*]. 'Tis false, Emperor !

Rufus. Silence, caitiff, or by heaven we will cut out thy false tongue ! The General has left the city, but before going he entrusted me with this parchment.

> [*Draws from under cloak.* EMPEROR *reads quickly.* CALPHURNIUS *wringing his hands, etc.*

" I Calphurnius, high-priest of the Capitol, swear and sign this oath with my blood, that I offered the throne of the empire to Placidus on condition he would persecute the Christians ; and I further swear never again to speak against this harmless sect.

> " Signed in blood,
>> " CALPHURNIUS."

Trajan. Perjured villain ! Shackle him—death by inches shall rid us of this pious impostor !

Epicurus. The pious Calphurnius! [*Makes gestures of piety and hypocrisy.*]

Rufus. And now, Sintulus, a reckoning with you. Behold a hypocrite, the more despicable because a soldier! This afternoon I heard him say he would rise to fame on the blighted name of Placidus. [*Drawing near.*] Sintulus, I had resolved when I heard this false speech to let this poniard taste thy worthless blood; but here, in the presence of our divine Emperor, whom every soldier loves, and for the honor of the military grade you bear, I will give you a chance for your life. [*Throws off cloak; shows himself to be Rufus fully armed. Drawing sword.*] Draw your sword, coward, and save while you can the life that is not worth keeping!

Trajan. Give it to him, noble Rufus; put the silence of death on his lying tongue.

[*They fight; furious fencing.* SINTULUS *lets sword suddenly fall, etc.* TABLEAU: RU-FUS *with foot on chest. Sword lifted about to cut off head. Curtain falls.*]

ACT II.

SCENE I.—*A garden, flower pots, etc. Summer-house at one corner. In the summer-house an old man leaning on a small table, apparently asleep, dressed poorly as a gardener. He is supposed to have a vision, which may be represented by a series of tableaux vivants, by small apartment in centre scene as in First Act. The* FIRST TABLEAU *will be the gardener. A fac-simile in get up. Stands in the act of astonishment in recognizing two Roman soldiers; they too with hands up, in act of recognition; soft music.* TABLEAU II. *Two young men are standing before a number of soldiers defying them to pass.* TABLEAU III. PLACIDUS *is standing between these two youths, and coming, as in the act of recognition, a female.* TABLEAU IV. *The Martyrdom of* PLACIDUS, *as represented in last scene. N.B.—These tableaux are very simple and produce a very marked effect. They are not so difficult as at first may be imagined. The tableaux should be managed by small children, who are simply trained to keep the one position. At the commencement, a pretty child, dressed to represent an angel, bearing a little wand, steals over and looks into summer-house ; waves both hands gracefully over the sleeping gardener, then repairs to centre of stage, and orders visions, without speaking, to appear. Must be moving about from summer-house to tableaux ; smiling, lively, etc. In case the above tableaux vivants are found to be too difficult, the scene may be performed without them. Gardener, whose name is* HORTENSUS, *rises from his reclining position, and commences to water some flowers. Pauses over a passion-flower ; takes one in his hand.*

Hortensus. Ah ! tiny monitor, thou preachest an eloquent sermon. Why wreathe thy beauty with these mysterious emblems of sorrow ? In thy petals radiant with gold and purple we read consolation ! They remind us that it is our privilege rather than punishment to follow in the steps of the King whose insignia of royalty were the thorns, the nails, the cross ! For fifteen years, with widowed heart and moistened eye, thy blossom has cheered me, and, now that you are bursting again into bloom, I feel thou whisperest a feeling stronger than resignation, for, like thee, my hopes are bursting from the leaves around them, and ere long will bloom in the realization of my joy !

[*A voice is heard outside calling* HORTENSUS.

Master. Hortensus !

Hortensus. Coming, master !

[*Meets master without leaving stage.   Master dressed as Indian planter.*

Master. Hortens ! how are the fuchsias getting on.   They looked so drooping yesterday I feared my darling long-tongued pink belles would have collapsed and—and died ! (*Affectedly*).

Hortensus. The warm breezes that blew from Sahara dried them up, but this morning they are better.

Master. You seem very partial to those pas-sion-flowers; you are always watching them, and I have frequently seen tears in your eyes as you stood over them.

Hortensus. Yes, worthy master ! they remind me of great mysteries ; that tiny flower distils a balm over my sorrow-stricken heart ; its nails, its wounds, its beautiful crown !

[*Seizes a passion-flower again, and remains gazing on it fixedly.*

Master. Hortens, I have often thought of ask-ing why a cloud seems ever to hang over your thoughts ; for years that you are now in my ser-vice you have never smiled. Your education, the gentility of your manners, and your fidelity so noble make me think, Hortens, you have seen better days. What stroke of fortune has forced thee to seek sustenance in menial employment ?

Hortensus. Kind master, the Power that has marked the course of the stars has shaped the destinies of men; he has been pleased to try me with deep affliction.

Master. Tell me, then, the cause of thy affliction.

Hortensus. Thy words bespeak sympathy; listen to the tale of a heart-broken father—torn by destiny from his wife, his children, and his country! I am a Roman citizen and a soldier of fortune! [*Master starts.*] In the Judaic wars I won my sword under Titus; the Emperor gave me the command of a division of horse. Fortune then made a toy of me—raising me to the highest honors, and then casting me down with violence from the giddy heights of my pride. By fortune, good master, I mean not the dark system of fatalism worshipped under this name in pagan mythology—I mean the paternal providence of Him who counts the hairs of our heads, who causes the tide of human vicissitude to ebb and flow—now in the storm, now in the calm. After my return from the Judaic wars, I was called in an extraordinary way to the knowledge of the Christian religion. That Spirit which illumined my soul with supernatural light cast me into the furnace of sorrow. My crucible is still heated, for Heaven knows there is still dross in my sinful nature. Some unseen power destroyed

my villas, my castle, my honor, and cast me, with
a young wife and two infants, on a sea of misfortune, fallen, penniless, ruined. [*Becomes abstracted for a moment.*]   To avoid the taunts of false
friends and the indignation of the Emperor, I fled
at night towards Ostia.   I found a small craft
about to sail for these shores.   With difficulty I
secured a passage, but an evil spirit entered the
heart of the captain.   When we came in sight of
land, the captain—whose crime Heaven forgive—
put me and my two boys in a small boat and sent
us on shore.   He immediately set sail under a
fair wind, tearing from me the only solace that
was left me in the dark hour of my trial.

[*Buries his face in his hands and weeps.*

Master. Thy story is a strange one ; thy cup
indeed bitter ; but go on, old man—I long to
hear the end of thy extraordinary history.

Hortensus. I clasped my little ones to my
breast, and, remembering my promise to the
Spirit that revealed itself to me in the Apennines,
I penetrated this lonely and deserted country in
search of labor and food, but other trials awaited
me.   On the third day I came to a deep and
rapid river.   I could not take the two children
with me across the stream, and arranged to bring
one first, then return for the other.   Scarcely had
I reached the opposite bank with the youngest,
when the screams of the other called me to see

him carried away in the mouth of a lion. I plunged into the seething torrent again to hasten to his rescue—a father's love would fight the king of animals in his own forest!

Master. Did you save the child?

Hortensus. Alas! my wearied arms faintly battled with the torrent a moment, and the lion disappeared. I plunged into the forest, and heard again the cries of a child calling for help; but they came from the other side of the river—my youngest child was seized by a wolf. [*Weeps.*] Blame not my tears, good gentle sir, for day and night those scenes are passing before my tortured brain. In my dreams I hear their last pitiful cries for help; like the colors of a landscape that blend in a picture, the desert, the torrent, and the forest shade dissolve from one another into a deep-blue sea, tossing on its restless bosom the white sails of a guilty craft.

Master. A stranger tale I never have heard; thou must have a stout heart, Hortens. Were thy lot mine, I should have long since driven a poniard to my heart's blood. In the regions of Pluto I would war against the gods; but tell me, hast thou ever heard of thy wife? Dost thou hope to meet her again?

Hortensus. This morning when kneeling in yonder summer-house, I heard a whisper as if from some gentle guardian spirit; it poured a balm on my troubled heart, and bade me look for the daylight that should follow my night of trial. This is the sad anniversary of my loss, and I am now in the hands of a high destiny, summoned by Him who maketh use of the little things of this world to confound the strong.

[*Remains looking towards heaven absorbed in prayer. In the meantime, two Roman soldiers enter* L. C., *engaged in conversation.* RUFUS *in same dress.* EGGEUS. *The same two that appeared in first scene.* HORTENSUS *looking up recognizes* RUFUS. *Starts ; but remains incog.*

Rufus. I tell you, Eggeus, I am sick and tired of this useless search. To-morrow I will return to Rome.

Master. Who are those strangers? What a curious dress? Whence come these people?

Eggeus. See, Rufus, there are persons here ; let us ask them if they know anything of the general.

Rufus [*advancing*]. Gentlemen, excuse our intrusion, but we come on important business from the Emperor. [HORTENSUS *starts.*] Know you of a man named *Placidus* in these regions?

Hortensus. Why seek you Placidus? Are you blood-hounds sent on the track of some hapless victim of imperial wrath?

Rufus [*aside*]. I know that voice; those haughty tones and majestic mien. [*Turning towards* HORTENSUS.] Sir, I should be the last man in the empire to be a blood-hound on the track of the great Placidus. We seek him, not to drag him to torture, nor to gratify with his murder any imperial revenge. We wish to put him once more at the head of the veteran legions of the empire. War has been proclaimed in the provinces. The troops are marshalling in the capital, but there is no one to lead them to battle. It was reported in Rome that Placidus is still alive, and the troops proclaim they will not serve under any other commander. The Emperor has promised a large reward to any one who will find out his retreat. The veterans who have served under him have gone in search to all the provinces. I, Rufus, who have borne his flag in the thickest of the fight, have sought him sorrowing through the parched plains and scanty villages of this miserable country. [HORTENSUS *betraying great excitement.*] Sir, your excitement seems to betray the knowledge of the great General. I command you, in the name of the Emperor, to point out his whereabouts, that we may communicate to him the glad tidings we bear.

Hortensus [*abstracted*]. From solitude to the din and clash of war! From obscurity to the laurels of the conqueror! Like sunrise on the darkened plains, the end intimated in prophetic whispers is bursting on my widowed heart in the realization of protracted hope. To arms! to triumph! the safety of the empire will be to me a *Double Triumph!* [*Turning towards* RUFUS.] Thou art a soldier, stranger. Hast thou not won some scars in fighting for thy country?

Rufus. Yes; by the side of our brave General I was wounded in the Judaic wars.

Hortensus [*showing cuts on arm, etc.*] Dost thou not see these scars? [*A moment's pause, then very loud.*] Rufus!

Rufus. Placidus!

[TABLEAU. *Curtain falls.*

————

SCENE 2.—*Scene in Arabia. Tent.* PLACIDUS *sitting on camp-stool at a small table. Near him* RUFUS. *A sentinel walking up and down in rear. Conversation between* PLACIDUS *and* RUFUS.

Placidus. How goeth the night-watch, Rufus; has the sun yet broken through the clouds on the horizon?

Rufus. Not yet, General; but the moon is bright.

Placidus. I don't like our position near these mountains, Rufus, and we will change the first thing by daylight. Just now I heard a deep rumbling sound like the distant tread of horses.

Rufus. When last I went around, all was safe. I heard the noise you speak of, but our Arab guide told me it was but the roar of the sea, which is not many leagues away. Not trusting this Arab slave, I have doubled the sentry guard. One of our scouts yesterday suspected treachery, and bade me tell you.

Placidus. It is well, Rufus! I remember me well how thy caution saved the Roman army under the battlements of Jerusalem. Forty winters have cast their snows on thy brow since then; yet thou hast not lost the fire of thy heart, nor the keenness of thine eye.

Rufus. When I was a pagan, good General, I knew of no god but my sword; I cared for no glory but that won in the carnage of the battle-field; I knew of no restraint but self-will; but since you made me a Christian, my actions are guided by a higher sphere of thought; I believe the greatest glory and the highest honor is the discharge of duty.

Placidus. Good, Rufus! Thou art as zealous in the young faith as thou are brave in thy veteran courage.

Rufus. What is the bravery of a soldier who has thousands ready to die with him in the ar-dor of battle, compared to the bravery of the defenceless Christians who voluntarily met death in its worst forms for the faith of Christ! I was present when Ignatius was devoured by the lions in the Coliseum; I saw gentle youths and tender virgins fearlessly await a similar doom, and, though yet a pagan, I longed for the glory of a death like theirs.

Placidus. Heaven will grant it to thee! [*Drawing near, makes some friendly gesture; e. g., the hand on his shoulder.*] Rufus, I had long wished for an opportunity to tell thee a secret committed to me by Heaven. As it has been mine to lead you on in the battles of the empire, it will be mine also to lead you to the scaffold of martyrdom. The sun of our career is fast setting on the troubled sea of time; the brilliancy of its sunset shall live in the memory of man longer than the fame of our conquests. The marble mausoleums of the pagan heroes shall long have crumbled to dust; the empire itself shall have disappeared, bearing but the memory of its magnificence, like the meteor that passes through the dark midnight sky; yea, the earth, the sun, the myriad worlds of the starry firmament, shall glide with a rapidity of thought to the dread chaos of original nothingness; but we shall ever be young in immortal youth, unhurt amid the war of elements, the wreck of matter, and the crash of worlds. Our souls, redeemed by the blood

of a God, are made heirs to an eternal king-
dom.

> [*A cry of " To arms!" " To arms!" is heard
> outside.* R. C. *Swords clash, trumpets sound,
> drums beat, and commands given by loud
> voices.* RUFUS *rushes out.* PLACIDUS
> *seizes battle-axe and describes what is pass-
> ing.*

Placidus [*loud*]. On, brave soldiers, on! [*Speaking to himself.*] Haste, Rufus, to the rescue!
Those noble youths! They fight like heroes!
The Pretorians are up! He has fallen! Victory
is ours now! They run! Thanks to the God
of armies! Trumpeter! [*Looking to the other
side.*] Sound a recall! Victory does not de-
mand the useless and cruel shedding of blood.

> [*Enter* TRUMPETER *and plays a beautiful
> military call.* RUFUS, *out of breath and
> without helmet, rushes in.*

Rufus. We were in a snare, but we have gained
a bloody victory—due to the bravery of two Numidian youths who stood alone against the whole
brunt of the enemy in the mountain pass. With
giant stroke they wielded their battle-axes, and
felled the enemy like saplings in a forest. I came
up with a division of horse just as their strength
was failing; but I fear they are sadly wounded.

Placidus. Bring hither those noble youths. Let

me tell them the gratitude of an army they have
saved, and an empire they have honored.   [*Lays
down his battle-axe. Puts on military cloak. Paces
stage. Suddenly stops. Sees youths coming.*] Ah !
young, beardless boys !   How noble — how hand-
some !   O my children ! would you not be like
those noble youths, had propitious destiny spared
you ! [*Enter two youths, military dress, bandaged,
covered with blood, leaning on the arms of others.*
RUFUS *supporting one.   They carry battle-axes,
also covered with blood.* PLACIDUS *advancing towards them.*]   Brave youths ! the empire owes
you a great debt.   Your bravery has saved thy
companions in arms from foul treachery.   Henceforth you must bear the rank of captain, and the
friendship of thy General.   Rufus, see to those
gallant youths.   I shall haste to the battle-field
to stay unnecessary bloodshed, and prepare the
march from this luckless mountain pass.

[*Exit* L. C.

Rufus. Be seated, young men.   You are weak.
[*Opens flask, pours out wine.*]   Drink to your victory !   and may Heaven give you many such
glories !   I felt all day yesterday we would soon
have some fighting. I saw a cloud on the brow of
that Arab guide.   In his bronze features I read
treachery and deceit ; but how came you to be
the first to see the enemy, and to be so close to
hand at the pass ?

Imogen [*the eldest*]. Kind Captain! yesterday evening when the sun was setting, my friend and I were strolling outside the camp, whiling away our time with tales of boyhood adventures, when suddenly we heard a rustling in the bushes near me. I drew my fleetest arrow and expected some startled doe to spring from its cover; another moment and it quivered in the heart of our Arab guide—the wretch who acted as our guide yesterday. Knowing he had come out on some foul mission of treachery, we watched to see if any caitiff would come to receive the message of this traitor. Night came on, and in the pale light of the moon we saw the swarthy figure of an Asiatic soldier glide from tree to tree and stealthily approach the Arab's hiding-place. Our trusty shafts drank his blood, but the wretch when dying gave a shrill whistle. We knew the enemy were at hand. We remained in the pass as sentries to give timely warning to the camp, and foil the treachery of cowards and slaves!

Rufus. How noble! how like the deeds of Roman heroes! Your names, young men, shall be bright on the pages of history. You must be descendants of Jugurtha or Hannibal, since you come from their country.

Imogen. No, kind Rufus. I, at least, am not a Jugurtha, nor yet am I a descendant of that brave General whose offspring even to this day swear hostility to the Roman Empire. You judge wrongly, Rufus, when you say I belong to the nation that was crushed by Scipio. Although here in the garb of a Numidian soldier, I have noble blood in my veins, and proudly call myself a Roman citizen !

"A Roman citizen !" [*Rufus and Farfax together.*]

Rufus [*aside*]. A Roman citizen ! Of noble blood ! Yet a common soldier in the Numidian corps. Perhaps the pain of his wounds has affected his head. He must surely be raving.

Imogen. My wounds are not so severe, Rufus, and my tongue is not so false; there can be no true greatness where there is deception.

Rufus. But say, what cruel circumstances have reduced a Roman citizen to be a mercenary in a Numidian corps?

Imogen. Spare me that word mercenary, for when thou hast heard my history thou wilt see that other motives besides gain have made me carry the axe and quiver of the swarthy and cunning Numidian. I promised Farfax I would tell him to-day some strange accounts of my childhood. Give me, and listen to a strange story. [*He drinks, and the others seated draw near him.*] My father was a soldier of fortune. By his bravery in the Judaic wars he was raised by the Emperor to the command of a division of horse. [RUFUS *starts.*]

Rufus. A master of horse?

Imogen. Yes.

Rufus. In the Roman army?

Imogen. Yes.

Rufus. By Trajan?

Imogen. Yes.

Rufus. Imogen—but go on; perhaps I am mistaken; but a strange suspicion is the harbinger of great joy.

Imogen. After the Judaic wars peace reigned in the empire, and my father lived in great wealth. One day he went to hunt, but came home late—he spoke of some strange adventure—he brought us to the Catacombs that night. A young man dressed in patrician costume met us in the street, and acted as our guide. We were brought through long subterranean passages to a small chapel beautifully lit up; the walls were covered by mysterious paintings, and a venerable old man with silvery beard sat in a stone chair. The old man seemed to know my father; he spoke some things that made my parents cry. We then passed through some ceremonies, by which I know I was made a CHRISTIAN.

Rufus. Each word falls like a drop into the vessel of my heart; it will overflow before he has finished his tale.

Imogen. Soon after this my father met with great adversity; his flocks died; his villas were burnt; he was persecuted by the Emperor, and one night, taking me and my mother and little brother, three years of age, he fled from Rome towards the port of Ostia. The captain of a craft about to sail to Africa gave us a passage; but he was a cruel, bad man, for when we came in sight of land he sent my father and my brother and myself on shore, and set sail again, bearing away my poor mother, whom I have never seen since. [*Buries his face in his hands, and weeps for a moment.*] I will never forget how my father wept, pointing with his trembling finger to the white speck the vessel had made on the blue horizon, and, clasping me to his breaking heart, said, " Your mother is gone with a stranger." Praying for strength to the God of the Christians, he sprang up, brushed away the tears, and took us with him into the country. We came up to a stream very deep and strong, and father, seeing he could not take both of us over together, left me on the bank whilst he swam across with my brother; he had just reached the other bank when out jumped an enormous lion from the trees, and took me in his great jaws and carried me into the forest.

Farfax. O Imogen! I have something to tell you when you are done; but how were you saved?

Imogen. Some shepherds seeing me in the lion's mouth set their dogs after him ; irritated by the dogs, the lion dropped me from his mouth, and took one of them instead. The shepherds took me to their house, and a good woman nursed me, for my side was all torn by the lion's teeth. I lived for fifteen years with these people. War being proclaimed in the East, I joined the forces, in the hope of getting back to Rome to find again my father and mother ; but Heaven knows where they are now.

Rufus. Noble youth, thy father still lives. [IMOGEN *rises*.]

Imogen. O Rufus ! say if he returned to Rome ; if old age and sorrow have made him a feeble wreck of manhood ; if he is in want ; if—

Rufus. He will answer for himself before sunset. I shall be the first to tell thy father of his joy. [*Exit*.

Farfax. O Imogen ! stay one moment.

Imogen. I must hurry, for Rufus seems to know my father ; he is alive ; he is in the camp.

Farfax. Whilst you were telling your story my heart was bursting to interrupt you to tell you that I believe I am your brother.

Imogen. Say how—are we in a dream ?

Farfax. I, too, am a Roman citizen and a Christian. I, too, was saved from a wild beast on the banks of the Chobar ; the people who saved me told me I was a Roman, and gave me this medal, which they said they found around my neck, and by it I know I am a Christian.

[*Draws out medal.*

Imogen. Show it ; has it got on it the figure of the cross and the Ides of March ?

Farfax. Yes; here it is !

Imogen [*seizing it, looking at it fixedly, draws another from his bosom*]. The medals the Pope gave us the night we were baptized. My brother Agapius !

[*They embrace.* TABLEAU. *Curtain falls.*

SCENE 3.—*The same. Tent in Arabia.* PLACIDUS *embracing his two children.*

Placidus. My children ! my children ! [*Pauses awhile, and then looks affectionately on them.*] Thrice this morning I felt some gentle spirit tuning the fibres of my heart for the music of joy ! Yes, beautiful, brave Christian ! Wert thou alive, Stella, how thou wouldst gaze with rapture on thy noble sons !

Imogen. Say, father, is mother really dead, or dost thou but fear that a broken heart brought her an early tomb ?

Placidus. Alas ! I fear the worst ; but whilst

yet I tread this valley of sorrow I hope again to meet thy mother, boy! This very morning the vision that passed before my soul placed thy mother in the embrace of her two sons.

Imogen [*passionately*]. Father, I shall travel the world till I find her, and if the wretch who tore her from thee still contaminate the earth of God, I shall steep my sword in his guilty blood!

Placidus. Hold, my child! Such language ill becomes a Christian. When young blood flowed in my veins, I could not sleep on an insult, but I have now learned to love and practise the sweet law of Him who has commanded us to love our enemies. I have long since forgiven that wicked man, who was but an instrument in the hands of Providence to try me in the crucible of misfortune.

Imogen. Such virtue, father, seems to me nobler than the qualities that make heroes seek the front of battle.

Placidus. Imogen, that law is divine, not human. When you were made a Christian on that strange night which marks an epoch in the memories of your childhood, you insensibly imbibed the golden stream of grace which nerves the soul to acts of self-denial, which is of a higher order than military courage. The soul is yet dimmed by a passing cloud. Yet a few days, and that soul will burst from its tenement of clay, like the rose from its bud, with the crimson effulgence of a Christian triumph. [*Is abstracted for a moment, and looks towards heaven.*] A triumph, Imogen, thou little dreamest of now !

[*Shouts are heard in the distance. All start and look in the direction.*]

Placidus. What mean those shouts ? Is Rufus here ? He is sure to know what is the matter.

Imogen. See, Rufus is running towards us. I am sure he has some good news to communicate. See how the dear old captain runs. Who is the stranger with him. There is surely something up.

[*Enter* RUFUS *and* COURIER *bearing despatches.* COURIER'S *pants stuffed into boots all covered with mud ; leather bag, etc., horn, etc.*

Placidus. Say, Rufus, what is the matter ? Those shouts ; your excitement. What has happened ?

Rufus. Good General, there is a courier from Rome. The Emperor is dead, and the army recalled. This courier has despatches for you.

[COURIER *kneels and hands large letters to* PLACIDUS.

Placidus [*reads*]. " It has pleased the gods to

raise us to the throne of the Empire. We de-
cree a triumph to the army of Placidus, and command our General to return forthwith to the
Capitol.

          " (Signed),   ADRIAN."

Placidus [*looking at the despatch.*] Strange
news! sad news! nay, glad news! Thou art
setting, thou brilliant sun of my hopes; those
grand destinies foreshadowed in prophetic whispers are gliding into realities. Ay! to Rome,
to triumph! to martyrdom! [*Remains abstracted.
Starting suddenly.*] Give orders to strike the
tents, Rufus, we march by daylight; go, Imogen
and Farfax, and superintend the preparations for
the march.   [*Exeunt.*

Placidus [*alone, and walking up and down the
stage.*] Ay! to triumph; to step from the golden
chariot to the tomb; to climb the glittering
heights of the Capitol amid the shouts that rend
the heavens with blasphemies against my God;
to kindle the fires of impure sacrifice to the demons of idolatry. Rather shall Placidus be cast
on the burning pile and be himself the victim!
In the dreams of my misguided ambition I
coveted the honor now within my grasp, but in
the light of the higher destiny that follows 'tis
but a beautiful shadow that floats before the in-
fatuated fancy like gilded bubbles on the stream

that break into thin air when we attempt
to seize them. My children, will you drink of
my cup? Will you ride in the same chariot till
we reach the atrium of the temple of Jupiter,
then be bound to the same stake, till the flames
of the funeral pyre send our liberated spirits to
the land of eternal triumph, where the shout of
real joy shall ring out the congratulation of
Heaven's choirs for our Christian victory? Poor
Stella! thy noble soul is still wanting to com-
plete the holocaust! Art thou pining away in
some villain's home?

> Perchance you died in youth, it may be bowed
> With woe far heavier than the ponderous tomb
> That weighs upon thy gentle dust—a cloud
> Might gather o'er thy beauty, and a gloom
> In thy dark eye prophetic of the gloom
> Heaven gives its favorites—early death.

Enter RUFUS.

Rufus. General, the poor woman on whose
ground you have pitched your tent wishes to
speak to you.

Placidus. Say, Rufus, I wish to be left alone.
If she wants money, take her this purse.

[*Exit with purse.* PLACIDUS *paces up and
down.* RUFUS *returns.*

Rufus. Sire, this old woman says she does not

want money [*returns purse*]; but begs an interview for a moment.

Placidus. Then see her in, Rufus.

[*Enter female, deeply veiled.*

Female [*kneeling*]. Great General of the Roman arms! will compassion move thee to pity a broken-hearted widow?

Placidus. 'Tis the privilege of those in power to protect the poor. Speak, good woman; has any one done aught to harm or injure thee?

Female. Permit me, I beseech you, to go, under your protection, to the land of my birth! I am a Roman matron! I was brought here for unlawful purposes, but I swear by the God who sees my innocence that I have never lost my fidelity to my husband. This day fifteen years ago I was torn from him by violence—

[PLACIDUS *starts several times. At these last words turns round to hide confusion. Female rises suddenly. Throws back veil, and with much vehemence :*

Female. Can it be? Do my senses deceive me? [*Rushes partly towards him.*] Say, art thou Placidus, the commander of the horse, who was converted in the Apennines; whose wife—

Placidus. Yes—yes! knowest thou of her? [*Recognizes her ; cries aloud—*] Stella!
Female. Placidus!

[TABLEAU. *In act of approaching to embrace. Curtain falls.*

———

SCENE 4.—*The Atrium of the temple of Jupiter on the Capitol at Rome.* EMPEROR *sitting on throne in porch. Procession of triumph passes before him. Children fantastically dressed, bearing spoils of conquered people ; some are carrying large bouquets of flowers. Dancing. Lively music. Small chariots drawn by goats may appear, etc. Get-up ad libitum. The last in the procession,* PLACIDUS—*if possible in chariot, gilt, drawn by pony, etc. Near* EMPE-ROR *an idol, a pan of incense, and a lamb covered with flowers, and vestal virgin. The high-priest.* PLACIDUS *advancing to the* EMPEROR'S *throne.* COURTIERS *cry out :*

" Hail, Conqueror, hail! "

Placidus [*presenting parchment tied with red tape*]. Behold, Emperor, the map of thy extend-ed territories!
Emperor. The gods have been propitious to

our arms, noble Placidus. Thy country has justly decreed for thee the greatest of honors. Ac-
cept the crown of victory given only to the
bravest of the brave. [*A vestal virgin. A little
girl dressed in white; advances, and, receiving
crown from* EMPEROR, *places it on the head of* PLA-
CIDUS.] Placidus, arise! the second place in the
empire is thine henceforth, together with thy
noble sons, of whose bravery we have heard so
much. You must live in our golden house. After
the hardships of the campaign you should now
enjoy the luxuries of your wealth and the splendors of your fame. And now [*rising*], brave
General, let us proceed to offer sacrifice to
Jupiter and Mars, who have been so propitious to the Roman arms! [PLACIDUS *remains motionless in pensive mood.* EMPEROR
turning suddenly round.] What, dost thou refuse
to follow? Are, then, the rumors of the people
and the accusations of the high-priest true?
[*Aloud and advancing.*] Placidus, dost thou refuse to do sacrifice to the gods of the empire—
to Jupiter who rules the destinies of man, and
given thee thy victories?

Placidus. Emperor! send me to the ends of
the world, to deepen rivers with the blood of thy
enemies; let me lead thy armies to the icy North,
or to the parched plains of thy African posses-
sions; command my sword, my wealth, my life;

but to bow to painted idols; to sacrifice to the demons of evil that hold the world in the thraldom of eternal perdition, I refuse!

Emperor. What infatuation has seized thee, Placidus? Callest thou our gods demons of evil? Dost thou not know I have power to force thee to sacrifice?

Placidus. I am perfectly aware thou hast no power but that which is given to thee from above by Him who created all things. Thy power, Emperor, is no greater than the power of the marble effigy thou callest Jupiter. He who alone is great could give life to the statue, as he has given it to thy body of clay.

Emperor. Dost thou say our noble person is made of clay? Has the pride of thy victories made thee insolent? Who is the God of whom thou speakest with so much infatuation? Is he the same that was crucified?

Placidus. Yes! in a mystery beyond the comprehension of man, our God was crucified!

Emperor. Placidus, art thou a Christian?

Placidus. Yes, thank Heaven, though unworthy of the great name.

High-Priest. "The Christians to the lions!"

All. "Away with the Christians!"

Emperor. Placidus, thy old age, thy bravery, thy merits, make me pity thy infatuation. Sacrifice to our immortal Jove, or by our piety I will tear thy laurels from thy brow, cast thee into a loathsome prison, and have thee die a miserable death like thy crucified God!

Placidus. Delay not to execute thy threats. My soul yearneth for the Cross! for death! for liberty! Let others enjoy the fleeting shadows of earthly triumph! Give me death for Christ, and you crown me with a DOUBLE TRIUMPH!

Emperor [*angry*]. Thou shall have it, then. Seize him, lictors! Prepare a scourge for this Christian!

> [IMOGEN *rushes in front with drawn sword.* FARFAX *also draws sword. Standing between them and* PLACIDUS.

Imogen. Dare you touch my father!

Placidus [*advancing*]. My son! put back thy sword! If thou lovest me, let them shackle me! Why stand between me and the crown I have sighed for? [*Rushes towards lictors. Places his hands in the chains. To Emperor*—] Now, tyrant, do thy worst! Wreak thy vengeance on this aged body, and free a captive spirit that longs for the freedom of the skies.

Imogen [*flinging down his sword with great noise*]. Father, I will die with thee. I, too, am a Christian! [*Moves towards him.*]

Farfax. So am I! [*And moves towards him.*]

Stella. And I believe in Jesus Christ!

[*They are bound with ropes. Attendants cry out :*

" Death to the Christians ! "

[*High-priest louder than others. In the same time a trumpet sounds outside. A* COURIER *rushes in.*

Courier. A message from the camp !

[RUFUS *enters, fully armed. Standing in amazement at* PLACIDUS *and family bound.*

Rufus. Brave General! has it come to this? Say but a word, and a legion of thy veterans will put this tyrant in thy place, and make you their king !

Emperor. Who are you, insolent soldier, that darest trifle with our commands and speakest treason in our presence ?

Rufus. 'Tis Rufus, the Christian soldier, and Captain of the Banner Guard, come to tell thee there is a mutiny in the army. They have heard of your unjust treatment of our General, and the murmur of ten thousand indignant soldiers rolls with threatening thunder around thy golden house. They will burn it to the ground and roast thee in its flames !

Placidus. Rufus, cool thy anger. By the hope that raises us from earth to eternity ; by the faith that sustains us; by the hardships we have borne together for forty years, permit me, I beseech you, to finish the mockery of human triumph by the immolation of myself at the altar of truth. [*Changes tone, and emphatically.*] Rufus! another battle awaits thee. Prepare thyself and the Christian soldiers of thy legion to follow us in a few days!

Emperor [*in a rage*]. Seize the traitor!

[*Some guards rush towards* RUFUS, *who suddenly turns around, and with stentorian voice, and hand on sword, cries:*

"Back, slaves!" [*Slowly retiring.*] Farewell, Placidus; we meet again!

[*Slaves remain, afraid to advance.*

Emperor. Cowardly dogs! I shall have thee hung by the heels before a slow fire. Lead those Christians to the stake instantly! Away!

[EMPEROR *remains in position with hand stretched out. Soldiers and lictors form guard around* CHRISTIANS, *who move with slow step—some seconds between each step. Curtain is falling.*

Last Scene.—*A scene in the Palatine Garden. Lights lowered. In centre of stage a raised platform, on which a stake. To this stake or board erect is tied* Placidus *; on either side, his wife and two children. Logs of newly cut wood placed around the pile and against the* Christians. *A strong light cast on them by mirror from above. Guards, rough-looking soldiers, just finishing preparations to burn the* Christians. *Guards around in file. One of the executioners sets fire to the pile. This is done by handfuls of incense thrown on a pan of coals concealed under the logs of wood. The smoke will give the appearance of fire. When the smoke has got thick, a noise of tramping is heard outside.* Rufus *and several Christian soldiers enter to save* Placidus. *Pagans and Christians fight.* Tableau. *Whilst fighting,* Rufus *beats two antagonists—leaps up on the pile—cuts the ropes that bind* Placidus, *but finds him dead.* Rufus, *holding the dead body of* Placidus *in his arms, pointing with his sword to heaven. Christian soldiers each standing over his fallen antagonist. Red lights, thunder, etc. Curtain falls.*

www.ingramcontent.com/pod-product-compliance
Lightning Source LLC
Chambersburg PA
CBHW031242260626
47169CB00007B/2418